Outcast

by

Narinder Dhami

Illustrated by Sue Mason

J FF

1773793

You do not need to read this page –
just get on with the book!

First published in 2007 in Great Britain by
Barrington Stoke Ltd
18 Walker St, Edinburgh, EH3 7LP

www.barringtonstoke.co.uk

ISBN: 978-1-84299-464-1

Printed in Great Britain by Bell & Bain Ltd

AUTHOR ID

Name: Narinder Dhami

Likes: Reading, football, cats, travelling

Dislikes: Celery, bad manners, deep water

3 words that best describe me:
Happy, busy, friendly

A secret not many people know:
I nearly drowned in a river when I was nine, (which is why I don't like deep water!)

ILLUSTRATOR ID

Name: Sue Mason

Likes: Cycling on my pink bike, trees, having clean teeth, forward rolls, sunshine, a good lip balm, my brilliant friends

Dislikes: Removing tangles, the smell of fried bacon, spitting, sleet, tingling lips from raspberry blowing, broken umbrellas

3 words that best describe me:
Susannah Jane Mason

A secret not many people know:
I have this dream a lot in which I can fly to tree height after eating pink custard powder from a tin

Contents

Chapter 1
My Life

I'm a killer.

I'm hard and I'm cool and I'm clever.

I see what I want and I go for it.

I'm the best killer in the world.
I never miss.

And right now I can see my victim on
the other side of the garden.

I'm creeping towards him very slowly and very softly. Then I'm going in for the kill.

One ...

Two ...

Three!

Missed him! He's flying away into that tree. Stupid bird!

Oh, well, I'll get him next time. And now I'm going to sit down and give myself a good lick all over.

Yes, I'm a cat! A cool, clever cat.

Did you think I was a human? I hope you didn't. I don't like humans.

I'm not just any old cat. My name's Riff. It's short for Riff-Raff.

I'm the James Bond of the cat world. I haven't got an owner so no-one tells me what to do.

I do what I like and what I like best is to be wild and free. That's why my black and white fur is scruffy and my ears are torn and I have lots of scars.

Sssh!

Listen!

What was that?

Oh, no! I just heard someone talking inside the house.

DANGER!

HUMANS!

I jumped up and my tail twitched.
I didn't know my way around this garden
because I'd never been in it before.

Quickly I ran over to a big bush.
I crawled under it to hide. I could see the
kitchen window was open, and I heard a
boy talking inside the house.

"Mum, I'm going outside to play," he
said. "Where's my red truck?"

"It's where you left it, Danny," said
Mum.

"Oh, thanks a *lot*, Mum," Danny said.
"You're no help at all!" He sounded fed up.

His mum laughed. She sounded nice.
"Don't you remember? The wheel came off

your red truck," she said. "You gave it to me to fix. Here it is!"

"Thanks, Mum!" Now Danny sounded happy. "You're the best!"

Then I heard the back door open. So I crawled further under the bush. These humans *seemed* OK, but it was a trick. Humans are like that. You can't trust them.

I never know what they're going to do next!

Once I was a fluffy little kitten. Everyone likes fluffy little kittens, right? Wrong! When I was only six weeks old, my human family dumped me at the animal home. But it wasn't so bad because they dumped my mum and my three sisters too. At least we were all together.

When I was older, I went to live with a new family. They had two children. They were good to me at first, but then the family had a new baby. After that they started having a go at me *all* the time.

Don't make a noise!

You can't go into the baby's room!

Don't lie on the baby's blanket!

Eek! Get that dead bird out of the house!

So I ran away. Now I live on my own and I never stay in one place for very long.

But the leaves are falling off the trees and winter is coming. I need somewhere to stay, just until the winter's over. I need free food and a warm bed. When it gets warm again and spring comes, I'll run away to somewhere new.

Maybe *this* place would be OK ...

I peered out from under the bush. Danny had come into the garden. He was carrying a plastic box and he tipped it out onto the grass. It was full of toy cars.

I watched. Danny began to push the cars up and down the lawn. Did Danny and his family already have a pet? I had to find out!

If they had a dog, forget it! I'd have to look somewhere else for a winter home.

If they had a cat, maybe I could bully it so that it ran away. Then I could move in.

If they had a goldfish, I could eat it. Then they'd need a new pet.

If they didn't have a pet, then here I was!

And if they got bored or cross with me, so what? I didn't care. When the winter was over, I'd be gone.

A girl came out of the house. She was a bit older than Danny, but she had the same dark hair and big brown eyes.

"Danny!" she shouted loudly.

Danny looked up from his cars. "What's wrong, Kim?" he said to her. "It wasn't me who broke your DVD player. I didn't touch it!"

"Oh, never mind about that!" the girl said. I knew now that her name was Kim. "I wanted to tell you something else. You know we've been asking Mum for years if we can get a pet ..."

"Yes," Danny replied. "And she always says wait and see."

"Well, I asked her again this morning and this time she said YES!" Kim yelled, a big grin on her face.

"Cool!" Danny shouted and jumped up. "So are we going to get a cat?"

Kim nodded. "Isn't that great?" she said.

Underneath the bush I began to purr.

I'd just found a new place to crash out for the winter!

Chapter 2
My New Family

I watched Kim and Danny as they talked. It was time to go and say hello to my new family!

I looked down at my dirty black and white coat. Maybe I'd better clean myself up a bit first.

I sat down and began to wash. But then I heard a noise behind me. What was it?

I got to my feet and growled. I showed my teeth. My fur stood on end. I was ready for anything!

A little black kitten was trotting towards me.

"Hello!" he said. His big green eyes were bright and friendly. "I haven't seen you around here before. I'm Samson."

"Samson!" I said with a sneer. "What a stupid name!"

"You can call me Sam," the kitten replied. He bounced over to me but I lifted my paw and gave him a biff with it. I didn't want to hurt him, but he needed to know who was the Boss!

The kitten jumped back. "What's your name?" he said.

"My name's Riff," I said. "And I'm the Boss around here. Now go away, kid. I'm busy."

Sam sat down and his eyes were big and hopeful.

"Didn't you hear what I said?" I snapped. "Buzz off!"

Sam's little black ears drooped. "I just want to play," he said sadly. "Do you live around here, Riff?"

"Maybe I do and maybe I don't," I said.

"I live just down the street," Sam went on. "My owner's name is Mrs Lee. She's lovely."

"Yes, she's nice to you because you're a cute little kitten," I said. "But it won't last."

Sam looked very puzzled. "What do you mean?"

"She'll get rid of you when you grow up and you aren't cute any more," I replied.

"No!" Sam looked at me with his big green eyes. He looked upset. "Mrs Lee would never do that!"

"Humans always do that," I said. "That's what they're like." I licked my paws and cleaned my whiskers. "Now get lost, kid. Like I said, I'm busy."

"OK, Riff." Samson began to crawl out from under the bush. "I'll go and play with Danny and Kim. They're my friends."

"Wait a minute!" I stamped my paw down on Sam's tail to stop him. "Did you say you know those two little pests?" I said. "I mean, those two lovely kids?"

"Oh, yes," said Sam. "I come to play with them when Mrs Lee goes shopping."

What Sam said was great news! If Danny and Kim saw that I was friends with Sam, they'd like me too!

"I'll come with you," I said. "I'd like to meet them."

"Great!" Sam grinned. "Come on then, Riff!"

And he bounced out from under the bush.

I looked down at my fur. I hadn't had time to clean myself up. But maybe it was good if I was dirty and looked like a stray. Then Danny and Kim would feel sorry for me. I ran out into the garden. Sam was sitting on the grass, and Danny and Kim were tickling him and stroking his ears.

"I have to look cute and friendly," I said to myself and I ran up to them. So I put on my best cute and friendly face.

Suddenly Kim saw me.

"Help!" she screeched. "There's a big, horrible cat in our garden and he's going to attack Sam! Come here, Sam. I'll save you!"

She grabbed the kitten and held him high up in the air.

"I'm not going to attack Sam, you stupid girl!" I yowled. "Can't you see? This is my *friendly* face!"

"It's OK, Kim," meeowed Sam. "This is my friend Riff."

Kim went on holding Sam close to her. She gave me a dirty look so I gave her one right back.

"Sam doesn't look scared," said Danny. "I don't think this cat is going to hurt him."

He bent down and stroked me. I didn't like it, but I purred. I had to *pretend* I liked it!

"Hello, boy." Danny tickled me under the chin. I *hate* it when anyone does that to me! "Where have you come from?"

I looked sad. I made my tail and my ears droop. I let out a sad meeow.

"I think he might be a stray, Kim," said Danny.

"Yes, he must be," Kim replied. "He's dirty and he smells!"

What a *cheek*! I do *not* smell!

"Hey, I've just had a great idea!" Danny said. He grinned at Kim. "Mum said we could get a cat. So why don't we have this one?"

Yes! Result!

But Kim looked shocked. "Danny, don't be silly!" she shouted. "I want a kitten! A cute kitten! Not a smelly old stray cat!"

See? I told you humans were all the same.

Just then their mum came out of the house.

"What's all this shouting about?" she asked.

"Look, Mum." Danny picked me up and took me over to her. I tried hard to look cute and cuddly and friendly. "We've found this stray cat. Can we keep him?"

"No, Mum!" Kim said crossly. "I want a kitten like Sam!"

Mum stroked my back. Her hands were soft and kind. She seemed OK. I was sure she'd let me stay! I put on my best sad face and looked up at her.

"Danny, we can't just *keep* this cat," she said. "He could be lost. He could be someone else's pet."

Thanks a lot, Mum, I thought. *She wasn't going to help my plan work.*

"Oh, Mum!" Danny looked upset. "Can he stay with us just for tonight?"

Mum shook her head. "You can't bring him into the house, love," she said. "But you can feed him if you like. I've got some fish in the fridge."

Fish! Yum yum!

"You wait here, Puss," said Danny. He put me down on the grass. "I'll get you something to eat."

"Can Sam have some fish too, Mum?" asked Kim. "But I don't want him to wait here with this cat. I'll bring him inside with us. Just in case something nasty happens!" And she glared at me.

I watched Danny and his mum go into the house. Kim went too. She was still holding Sam.

I could tell that Danny liked me. And I could see that his mum was kind. She'd let me stay if she knew I was a stray.

But I had a problem. A big problem.

And her name was Kim!

Kim wanted a kitten, but I wasn't going to let that stop me. Oh, no.

I had an idea!

Chapter 3
My Brilliant Plan

Danny gave me some fish and milk. He brought it into the garden in an old red plastic bowl. Then I played with him for a little. I didn't want to play with him. But I wanted him to like me so much that he would *beg* his mum to let me stay.

I tried to be nice to Kim, but she kept away from me. She wouldn't even stroke me! Silly girl! She didn't know that cats are

very clever, and humans are stupid. But I'd show her!

Then Danny and Kim went in for tea. So I curled up under the bush and had a long nap. Sam ran off home.

When it was dark, I woke up. Time to put my plan into action!

There was a water butt underneath the windows. It was one of those tall green barrels where you can store rainwater from the gutters. It didn't have a cover but I jumped up onto the rim. I needed to look inside the house. I peered into the kitchen. The door was open and I could see Mum and Dad in the living-room. They were sitting on the sofa, watching TV. I couldn't see Danny and Kim. It was late. Maybe they'd gone to bed.

I was looking for a way into the house. I had to get inside!

That was my plan. And then I was going to creep upstairs and sleep on Danny's bed. I knew that Danny'd let me stay on his bed until morning. Once I got inside the house, I could make myself at home. I was sure Mum would let me stay.

If she put me outside, I'd get into the house the next night. And the next. And the next. I'd keep getting inside until they let me stay. And Kim would just have to put up with it!

I looked up at the back of the house. The big kitchen windows were closed. I jumped down from the water butt and walked along the side of the house. I kept my eyes open and kept hunting for a way in.

Then I saw that a very small window was open. Could I jump high enough to get in there?

"Here we go, Riff," I said to myself. "One ... Two ... Three –"

Just as I was about to jump, Sam the kitten came padding towards me.

"Hello!" he mewed.

"Where did you come from?" I snapped. "Get lost, kid. I'm busy."

"You always say that," Sam replied. He sat down next to me and I glared at him. This kitten was starting to annoy me! "What are you doing?" he said. He couldn't even see I was annoyed.

"I'm going into the house," I said. I nodded at the open window. "If I can get inside, then they'll feel sorry for me. If they feel sorry for me, then they'll let me stay!"

"Danny likes you," said Sam. "But what about Kim?"

I twitched my whiskers. "What about her?" I replied. "She can get a kitten after I've left and gone somewhere else."

Sam looked puzzled. "What do you mean?" he asked.

"I'm only staying for the winter," I said. "Then I'll move on."

"Move on?" Sam looked puzzled.

"Yes, move on," I said. "This house is just like a hotel. I'll stay for a bit. Then I'll leave and go somewhere else. That's what I do."

"No!" Sam's big green eyes opened big and wide. "How can you do such a thing? It's horrible! Danny will be so upset!"

"Am I bothered?" I said, with a yawn. "Once I've gone they'll get a kitten and then they'll forget all about me."

"I think you're mean," Sam said.

"Oh, do you?" I glared at him and showed my teeth. "Why don't you just buzz off home and leave me alone?"

Sam looked a bit scared. He jumped back and almost fell over.

"I still think you're mean!" he mewed. And then he ran off, with his little tail stuck up in the air.

Like I care what you think! I said.

Quickly I jumped up onto the windowsill. Then I squeezed through the open window. It was a tight fit but I just made it.

The window I jumped up on was the one for the downstairs toilet. I jumped down and padded softly out into the hall. I could hear the TV as I walked past the living room.

I went up the stairs and onto the landing. There were a lot of doors. I stopped and sniffed the air. Where was Danny?

The door next to me was open a little. I could hear people talking. So I pushed the door open wider with my nose and went in.

The room was in darkness, but there was a TV in there and it was on. I looked up at the screen. I could see a man in a big black cloak. He had long white teeth and he was biting someone's neck. He didn't look very friendly.

I could see that there was someone in the bed on the other side of the room. So I crept over to it. I jumped up and landed right on top of the duvet.

"Danny?" I mewed loudly.

"Help!" Kim screeched. "Help! The vampire's come to get me!"

Chapter 4
My Present

"Oh, no!" I meowed. "It's Kim's bedroom, not Danny's!"

I jumped off the bed and ran out onto the landing. Then I hid behind a tall plant in a big pot. Things were going wrong! This wasn't part of my plan! But maybe Kim hadn't seen me ...

Mum and Dad ran up the stairs and into Kim's bedroom. They didn't notice that I was hidden behind the plant pot. Danny came out of his bedroom, looking very sleepy, and he went into Kim's room too. I listened hard. I could hear everything they were saying.

"Why did you scream, Kim?" asked Mum. "And why aren't you asleep? It's very late."

"What's this on the TV?" Dad sounded very angry. "Are you watching a horror film, Kim?"

"You naughty girl, Kim!" said Mum. "You know you aren't allowed to watch scary films!"

Danny was laughing. "You're frightened of the vampire in the film, aren't you Kim?" he asked.

"I *wasn't* scared of the film!" Kim said loudly. "It was that stupid stray cat! He jumped up on to the bed and scared me!"

Oh, no! Quickly I slid out from behind the plant pot and ran off down the stairs.

"Well, you shouldn't have been watching a horror film anyway," Dad went on. "I'm taking your TV away for two weeks, young lady!"

I didn't hear any more. I shot downstairs and jumped out of the toilet window. I ran off to hide under the bush. Sam was sitting there in the moonlight.

"Your plan didn't go so well then?" he said.

"That won't stop me," I snapped.

I hoped Mum and Dad didn't blame me. They wouldn't let me stay if they were angry with me. But it was Kim that was my real problem now. She'd lost her TV for two weeks. So she was going to hate me even more ...

Next morning I sat by the back door. I was waiting for Danny to give me some breakfast. Maybe he'd forgotten about me already. I know what humans are like!

But then the door opened.

"Hi, Puss!" Danny came outside in his pyjamas. He had a dish in each hand. "Here's your fish and milk."

I rubbed my head against his legs quickly and began to eat.

"Kim's in a real mood," Danny said, and he gave my back a stroke. "I don't think she likes you very much, Puss!"

I looked up from my food. Kim was stomping round the kitchen. She opened the door of the fridge and slammed it shut. Then she looked and saw Danny and me in the garden.

"Watch out, Kim!" Danny shouted. "The vampire's coming to get you!"

Kim looked hard at us. Then suddenly she gave a screech.

"What's that?" she asked.

"What?" asked Danny.

"There!" Kim yelled. "By the back door!"

Oh, good! They'd found my present at last!

Danny took a look.

"I think it's a mouse's head," he said.

"A MOUSE'S HEAD!" Kim shouted. "You mean it's just a head? Where's the rest of it?"

"Well, I ate it, of course!" I said but Kim and Danny didn't understand. "Did you think I was going to give you all of it? You humans are so selfish!"

"Mum! Mum!" Kim was screaming her head off. "That horrible stray cat's left a mouse's head in our garden!"

Mum came out to see. She didn't scream or make a fuss. I think she loved my present!

"Cats like to catch mice, Kim," Mum said. "You'll have to get used to that if you want a kitten."

"Sam doesn't catch things!" said Kim.

"Sam couldn't catch a cold!" I said, "He's not a real cat!"

"I think Puss left it for us as a present." Danny stroked my ears. "He was saying sorry for last night."

"You're right, kid," I said. "You're not as stupid as you look!"

"Well, I think it's horrible!" Kim snapped. "Just keep that nasty cat out of this house!"

And she stomped out of the kitchen.

"Get over it, Kim!" I said, as I licked up all the milk. "I'm moving in, whether you like it or not!"

After breakfast I played with Danny for a bit. He pushed his cars up and down the grass and I ran after them. It was quite good fun. Well, it was fun if you like that sort of thing. I was just *pretending* to have fun.

When Mum called Danny in for lunch, I went off for a walk around the house. The front garden was very sunny so I lay down by the gate. Time for a nice snooze in the sun! I was just falling asleep when someone called my name.

"Hello, Riff," Sam mewed.

"Oh, no!" I yawned. I opened my eyes. "Not you again!"

"Don't go to sleep," said Sam. "Let's play a game!"

"No, thank you," I replied. "You said I was mean. So why do you want to play with me?"

"I think you *pretend* to be mean." Sam stared hard at me with his big green eyes. "But I don't think you *are* mean really."

"I *am* mean!" I said in a cold hard way. "I'm nasty. I'm horrible. I'm evil!"

Sam laughed.

"No, you're not," he said. "You're my friend."

I didn't say anything. I wasn't his friend. I don't have any friends.

Sam looked out at the street. "Who's that?" he asked.

I turned to see.

A big white van had stopped right outside the front gate. It had some letters on the side. *Greenside Animal Home* they said.

"Oh, no!" I mewed. "They've come to take me away!"

Chapter 5
My Escape

"Who's come to take you away?" Sam asked me.

"The animal home!" I said. "Danny's mum and dad must have rung them up because they think I'm a stray!"

A man got out of the van. He went round to the back of the van, and took out a big steel cage. Then he walked towards the

front gate, just where Sam and I were sitting.

"See?" I said to Sam. "I've got to get away!"

"Come on!" Sam gave me a push with his nose. "You'd better hide in the back garden!"

Sam and I raced off as the man came up the path towards the house. We ran round the side of the house, climbed over the side gate, ran along the fence and jumped down onto the grass in the back garden. Just then, the back door opened. Dad was standing there with the man from the animal home.

"Thank you for coming, Mr Moon," said Dad. He looked down into the back garden. "We don't know for sure that the cat's a stray. He could be lost and his owner could be looking for him. That's why we called you."

"Quick, Riff!" Sam panted. "Hide!"

"Don't tell me what to do!" I snapped. "I know how to get away from him. I've done it lots of times!"

I ran over to the bush and crawled into the middle of it. Sam crept after me. I glared at him but he didn't move.

We sat there as Dad, Mum, Danny and Kim all came outside. So did Mr Moon, the man from the animal home. We didn't make a sound.

"Have you seen the cat this morning?" asked Mr Moon, as he put the cage down on the grass.

"No," Danny said quickly.

"Yes, we have!" Kim cut in. "Danny gave him some breakfast."

I peered through the leaves. I could see that Danny was glaring at his sister.

"Where does the cat like to sleep?" Mr Moon put on a thick pair of gloves. Then he bent down and unlocked the cage. "Do you think he could be somewhere in this garden?"

"He likes to sleep down there," said Danny and he pointed at the bottom of the garden. But I never slept there because it was muddy and damp.

"Danny's trying to help!" Sam whispered in my ear. "He's trying to keep the man away from you!"

"Shut up!" I snapped. I didn't *want* help. I'd do this my way!

"No, he doesn't sleep at the bottom of the garden, Danny!" Kim snapped. "He likes to sleep in that bush right there!"

And she pointed at the bush where I was hiding.

"Go, go, go, Riff!" Sam mewed. He tapped me with his paw. "I'll hold Mr Moon off so you can get away!"

Stupid kitten! What could he do? But I crawled out from the other side of the bush and ran across the garden. Then I hid behind a large pile of leaves and watched.

Sam was scratching around in the bush, making a lot of noise.

"I can hear something!" said Mr Moon. "I think I've found your stray cat!"

He bent over the bush and pulled the branches apart. Then he lifted Sam up into the air.

"Got him!" he said.

"That's not the stray cat!" said Mum. "That's Sam. He belongs to our neighbour, Mrs Lee."

Mr Moon put Sam down on the grass and began looking around again.

"Maybe the cat's sleeping in another garden," said Danny. "Or maybe he's gone home."

"What's that?" Kim said suddenly. "I can see a cat's tail sticking out from behind that pile of leaves!"

Mr Moon came towards me. I growled. I made all my fur stand up on end. I didn't know which way to run!

"Good boy!" said Mr Moon. He bent down over the pile of leaves. "Pretty kitty!"

Pretty kitty! Nobody calls me pretty kitty and gets away with it!

As Mr Moon made a grab for me, I shot off across the garden. He fell over and landed head first in the pile of wet leaves.

"There he goes!" shouted Kim.

"Shut up, Kim!" said Danny.

I ran round the garden, looking for a way out. Then I saw Sam waving his paw at me.

"Quick, Riff!" he shouted. "There's a hole in the fence over here!"

Mr Moon got up. He was covered in wet leaves. But he began to chase after me, and he wasn't far behind. I raced towards Sam who was standing by the fence. There was a hole between two of the wooden planks.

"Go and hide in the garden next door!" Sam said, "Mr Moon will never find you there!"

The hole in the fence wasn't very big. I squeezed my way through it just as Mr

Moon came up behind me. He grabbed at my tail and missed.

"Help!" Mr Moon groaned, trying to pull his arm out of the hole. "I'm stuck!"

Ha ha! I'd escaped!

Mr Moon would never catch me now!

I looked around the garden. There was a big shed, so I ran and hid behind it. But I could hear everything that was going on next door. Mr Moon was stuck. Dad had to get his saw and cut a hole in the planks in the fence so Mr Moon could get his arm out. I stayed in the next door garden until I heard the van drive away. Then I crept out.

I went and looked through the hole. No-one was outside now except Danny and Sam.

I squeezed through the fence and ran over to them.

"Riff!" Sam yelled. His face lit up and he began to purr loudly.

"Hello, Puss!" Danny said. He was smiling too. "You're a clever old cat, aren't you? You got away from Mr Moon!"

Sam began to lick my face and Danny stroked me. I began to purr.

Stop!

Wait!

This wasn't right!

Chapter 6
My Friends?

What am I doing? I said to myself. *I'm mean! I don't make friends! I don't need friends! I don't like anyone!*

Sam and Danny had helped me to get away from Mr Moon. They were my friends now.

But I wasn't *their* friend.

I pushed away from Danny. I walked away from him and Sam, and went over to the bush. I sat down and began washing myself.

"What's the matter, Puss?" asked Danny. He sounded upset. But that wasn't *my* problem.

I yawned. Danny held out his hand but I didn't go to him. OK, so he'd helped me – but I didn't ask him to, did I?

"Danny!" Mum was shouting from inside the house. "Come in and tell me what you want for tea, please."

"I'll see you later, Puss," Danny said. "And I'll ask Mum and Dad again if we can keep you."

He waved at me and went inside.

"What was all that about?" asked Sam.

"I don't know what you're talking about," I said.

"Why did you walk away from Danny?" Sam wanted to know.

"Oh, humans are so boring." I yawned again. "I'm sick of them all!"

I knew what I had to do.

I had to leave. Right now.

Why? Because I was getting SOFT! I was starting to like Danny and Sam. That wasn't right. So it was time to go.

I went over to the water butt under the window. I jumped up onto the rim and looked inside the house. Danny was talking to his mum in the kitchen. He didn't see me but I didn't care. It wasn't like I wanted to say goodbye.

"What are you doing, Riff?" Sam jumped up onto the water butt next to me. He wobbled a bit as he stood on the rim beside me.

"I'm just having a drink of water before I leave," I said.

"Leave?" Sam stared at me. He was very upset. "Why? Where are you going?"

"Oh, I don't know," I said. "But I'm off. See you!"

"You can't go, Riff." Sam's little face was sad, but that wasn't going to stop me. "Danny will miss you, and so will I."

"Sorry, kid." I jumped down from the water butt. "When I go, I don't look back. And I'm going now." I turned and began to walk away. "Goodbye."

Splash!

I stopped.

I said that when I go, I never look back.

But that loud splash could only mean one thing.

I looked round.

Sam had fallen into the water butt!

Chapter 7
My New Home

I ran back and jumped up onto the rim of the water butt. Sam was splashing about in the deep, deep water, trying to keep afloat. He looked scared to death.

"Hold on, Sam!" I shouted, "I'll help you!"

I dug my claws into the edge of the water butt so that I didn't fall in myself. Then I bent over and grabbed Sam by the scruff of his neck with my teeth.

My plan was to pull Sam out of the water. But his fur was soaking wet and that made him really heavy. I tried to lift him up. I tried again and again, but I couldn't.

I felt very frightened. I couldn't let go of Sam or he'd drown. But he was too heavy for me to lift out of the water. I didn't know *what* to do. So I just hung on. I wasn't going to let go!

Suddenly I felt someone grab me tightly round my tummy.

"Don't worry," said Kim. "You're both safe now!"

She held on to me and pulled Sam out of the water with her other hand. Then she put us both down on the grass. Sam was soaked and shivering.

Danny and his mum had looked out of the window and they'd seen what was happening. Now they came running out of the house.

"What's going on?" asked Danny. "Why is Sam all wet?"

"I heard a splash and came to see what it was," Kim said. "Sam had fallen into the water butt and the stray cat was trying to save him. He's a hero!"

And she patted me on the head.

"Yes, you're a hero!" said Sam and he licked my nose.

Oh, *please*! I hate fuss! I pulled away and began to try and smooth down my damp coat.

"Look at me!" I grumbled. "I'm all wet from you splashing about, Sam!"

Sam just laughed. The cheeky little thing!

"So you *do* like me, Riff!" he said. "You said you never looked back. But you did, because you were worried about me!"

"I *wasn't* worried!" I snapped.

"Mum, *please* can we keep him?" Danny asked, picking me up. "I'm *sure* he hasn't got a home to go to."

"What about Kim?" said Mum. "She wants a kitten."

Kim smiled. "A cute little kitten couldn't have saved Sam like this dirty old cat did!" she said. "I'll give him a bath and then I don't mind if we keep him!"

A bath? *No way!*

"Well," said Mum, "we'll ask around and see if we can find his owner. If he really is a stray, then he can stay!"

"Thanks, Mum!" Danny said. He had an enormous grin all over his face.

"Welcome to your new home, Puss!" said Kim. She tickled me under the chin. I *hate* that! "But we can't keep calling you 'Puss'," she went on. "We'll have to give you a name."

"I want to call him Winston," Danny said.

Winston? That's a bit of a posh name for a dirty old stray cat like me! But I think I can live with it!

Oh, well. Maybe I *will* stay, after all.

Just for a bit.

I mean, these humans think I'm the best thing ever. What a bunch of suckers!

So I guess I might as well stick around ...

Barrington Stoke would like to thank all its readers for commenting on the manuscript before publication and in particular:

Annie Bristow
Ciara Gibbons-Coyle
Kirsty Johnston
Kirstine McCallum

Become a Consultant!

Would you like to give us feedback on our titles before they are published? Contact us at the email address below – we'd love to hear from you!

info@barringtonstoke.co.uk
www.barringtonstoke.co.uk